The Tooth Fairy and The Tooth Mouse

- A Tale About Culture Shock

Authors: Ariatna G. Claudio and Almaris Alonso-Claudio, Ph.D.

Illustrated by QBN Studios

Dedication

To children who lose teeth, whether they are visited by the tooth fairy or the mouse.

—Ariatna G. Claudio

To parents who nurture our childhood memories.

—Almaris Alonso-Claudio, Ph.D.

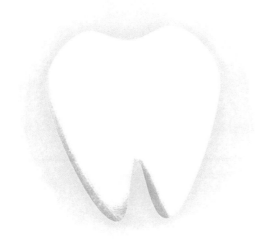

This book belongs to: _

Who visits your house—the tooth fairy or the mouse?

_ _ _ Tooth Fairy   _ _ _ El Ratoncito

Vocabulary

Buenas noches	Goodnight
Mucho gusto	Nice to meet you
Tengo una idea	I have an idea
Vamos a compartir	Let's share
El diente	the tooth
Gracias	Thank you
El Ratoncito	the little mouse

The Tooth Fairy and the Tooth Mouse
—A Tale About Culture Shock

First edition

www.thoughtsandwonder.com

Edited by: Marlo Garnsworthy, Icebird Studio

Illustrations: QBN Studios

Children's Fiction

Lucy was the happiest kindergarten girl in Maryland.
And soon, she would lose her first tooth!

One day at lunchtime, while eating an apple, Lucy noticed her loose tooth had gotten stuck on it.

"Ouch!" said Lucy, surprised. She showed the apple with her tooth to her friends.

"That's great, Lucy!" said Liam.

"Did you know that if you put the tooth under your pillow tonight, the tooth fairy will come and leave money for you?" said Melody.

"Is that true?" asked Lucy.

"Yes, it's true," said Melody.

"I can't wait to tell Mama and Papa," said Lucy.

But when Lucy showed Mama and Papa her tooth, and told them about the tooth fairy, they seemed confused. "A tooth fairy?" asked Mama in disbelief. "In Puerto Rico, we have a tooth mouse," Papa said, smiling.

Now, Lucy was confused.

"Why does a tooth fairy in Maryland have the same job as a mouse in Puerto Rico?" asked Lucy.

"Lucy, in some Spanish-speaking parts of the world," said Mama, "a mouse, not a tooth fairy, leaves money when kids put their tooth under their pillow."

"But we speak both English and Spanish at home," said Lucy.

"So, who will visit our home tonight—the tooth fairy or the mouse?"

"Maybe both!" said Mama, smiling.

That night, Lucy placed the tooth under her pillow and fell asleep, a bit confused. "Who will show up tonight—the tooth fairy or the mouse?"

That night, Lucy woke to a sound inside her room...
Flap, flap, flap, flap—it was the fluttering of wings!
Lucy opened her eyes to see a fairy in a white dress, with clear, long, glittery wings and wavy hair.
"You are the tooth fairy," she said.

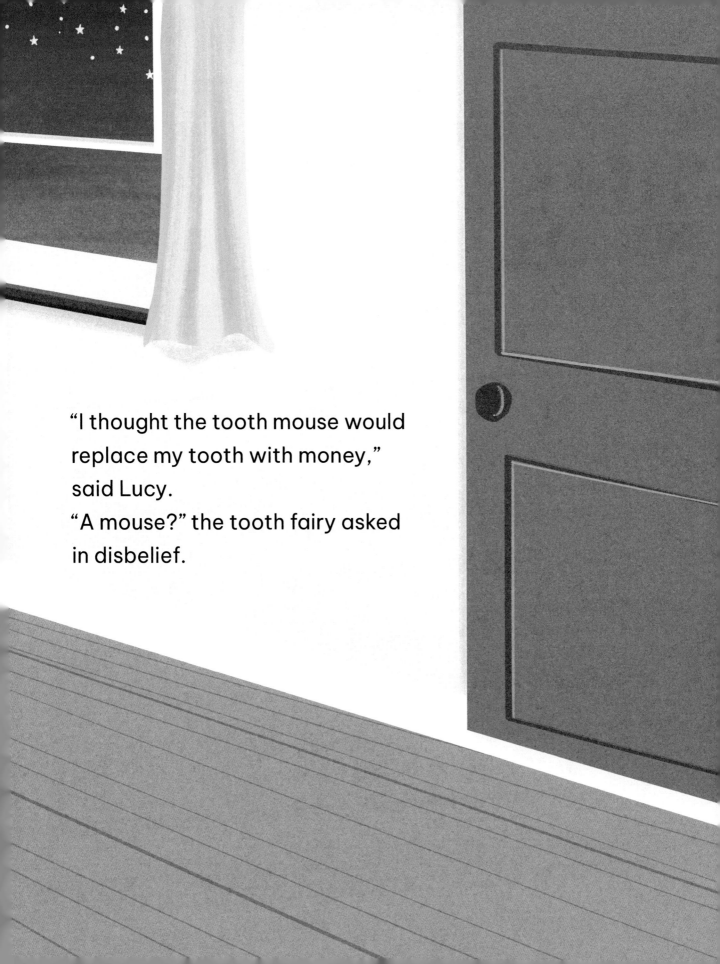

"I thought the tooth mouse would replace my tooth with money," said Lucy.
"A mouse?" the tooth fairy asked in disbelief.

Suddenly, Lucy heard another sound.
Squeak, squeak!
Lucy and the tooth fairy hugged each other as a
shadow appeared in Lucy's room.
"Ahhhh!" they yelled.

"*¡Buenas noches!*" said the mouse standing in Lucy's room. "Lucy, aren't you supposed to be sleeping? And who is she?" he said, pointing at the tooth fairy. "Noises woke me, and she is the tooth fairy who'll take my tooth and leave me money," said Lucy, surprised to see them both in her room.

"*Mucho gusto en conocerla,*" said the tooth mouse. "Nice to meet you, too," said the tooth fairy. Then she was curious. "Which of us is keeping Lucy's tooth tonight?"

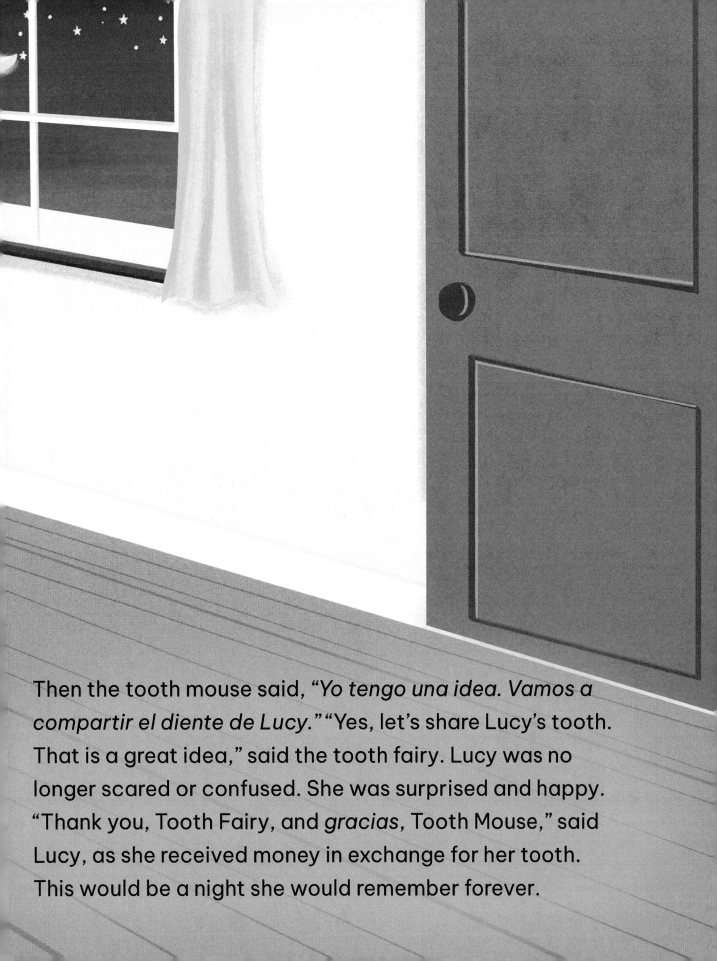

Then the tooth mouse said, *"Yo tengo una idea. Vamos a compartir el diente de Lucy."* "Yes, let's share Lucy's tooth. That is a great idea," said the tooth fairy. Lucy was no longer scared or confused. She was surprised and happy. "Thank you, Tooth Fairy, and *gracias,* Tooth Mouse," said Lucy, as she received money in exchange for her tooth. This would be a night she would remember forever.

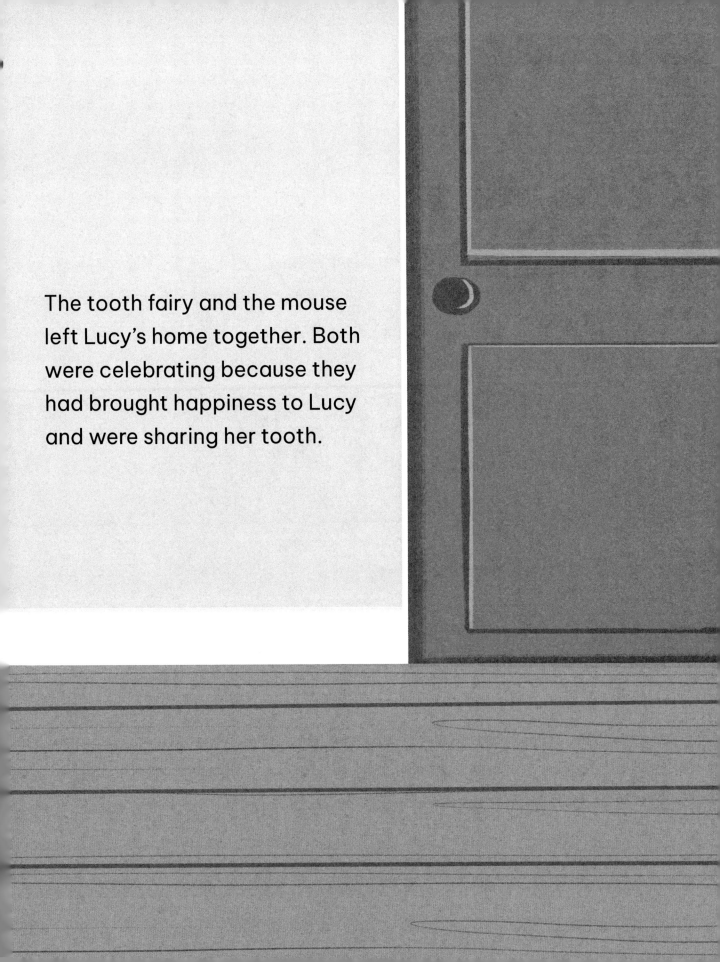

The tooth fairy and the mouse left Lucy's home together. Both were celebrating because they had brought happiness to Lucy and were sharing her tooth.

But they learned something that night—that they were not that different after all. The tooth fairy and the tooth mouse started to travel together, cheering children around the world. From each place they visited and with each memory they made together, they sent a postcard to Lucy. And each time Lucy received a postcard, she yelled, "I am so happy!"

Ariatna G. Claudio is a first-grade student with interest in themes of inclusiveness and diversity. Her role promoting empathy in the world has translated to her first children's book; The Mean Flower - a story about: The Power of Empathy (Spanish edition: La Flor Rebelde, una historia sobre el poder de la empatía). She was five years old when she developed this fascinating story. She enjoys gymnastics, horseback riding, swimming, creative writing, reading, drawing, and spending time with her family.

Almaris Alonso-Claudio is a mom, a wife, a scientist, an inclusive leader, an entrepreneur, and a children's book author. She attended public schools in Puerto Rico and finished a bachelor and a master's degree at the University of Puerto Rico in Mayagüez, a Ph.D. at the University of Massachusetts-Amherst, completed her Postdoctoral training at Harvard Medical School in Boston, and the leadership, diversity and inclusion certificate from Cornell University. Her work promoting equity and inclusion has been recognized with; The Woman Who Makes a Difference Award (UMASS-Amherst); The SACNAS Presidential Award; and The Excellence in Equity Award, presented by the Boston Executive Board. Her children's books promote inclusiveness, appreciation, respect, empathy, and acceptance. Almaris enjoys traveling with her family, trying new cultural-traditional recipes from around the world, cooking, reading, swimming, and mentoring students in STEM disciplines.

Published children's books: The Mean Foal a story about respect, mutual appreciation and acceptance (Spanish edition: El Potrillo Rebelde una historia de respeto, aprecio mutuo y aceptación); and The Mean Flower, a story about the power of empathy (Spanish edition: La Flor Rebelde, una historia sobre el poder de la empatía).

Made in the USA
Middletown, DE
19 October 2022

12905379R00020